Conte KU-016-016

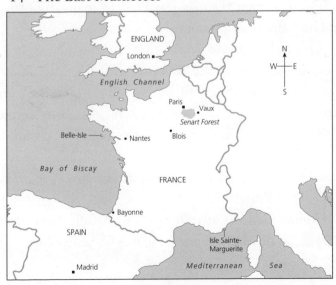

A Note About the Author

Alexandre Dumas was born on 24th July 1802, in Villers-Cotterêts, in northern France. His father was an important soldier – a general in Napoleon's army. Dumas' mother was the daughter of an innkeeper.

In 1823, Dumas went to Paris. He wanted to become a lawyer. But he worked in the house of a rich man. Dumas started to write historical plays and novels. They were exciting and they were successful. Dumas became a famous man. He was one of the most popular French writers of the nineteenth century. He liked good food, fine wines and beautiful women. Dumas travelled to many countries and he spent a lot of money.

Alexandre Dumas wrote three stories about some French soldiers in the seventeenth century. These stories are: *The Three Musketeers* (1844), *Twenty Years After* (1845), and *The Viscount of Bragelonne* (1844–1850). Other famous stories are: *The Count of Monte Cristo* (1844–1845) and *The Black Tulip* (1850). *The Man in the Iron Mask* is part of the story, *The Viscount of Bragelonne*.

Dumas died on 5th December 1870 at Puys, near Dieppe, in northern France. He was 68 years old.

A Note About This Story

Time: 1661.   **Place:** France.

In 1643, Louis XIV became the King of France. But he was only five years old. Queen Anne, Louis' mother, ruled for him until 1661. After that, Louis began to rule France himself. Nicolas Fouquet was Louis' Chief Minister of Finance. Jean-Baptiste Colbert was also an important adviser. The two men hated each other. Colbert and King Louis made France a rich and power-ful country. Louis ruled France for 27 years. He spent a great amount of money and he fought many wars.

In 1661, Louis saw Fouquet's house near Vaux. Then the king wanted a fine house of his own. He built a beautiful palace at Versailles. The work took more than 20 years.

This story is about four friends – D'Artagnan, Aramis, Porthos and Athos. They first met in 1625. They were soldiers in the King's Musketeers. 'All for one, and one for all!' – that was their promise to each other. For three years, they had many adventures together. Then Athos, Porthos and Aramis left the musketeers. After that, Athos lived in a house near Blois. Porthos married a rich lady and he lived in Paris. Aramis became a priest, and later he became the Bishop of Vannes. D'Artagnan became the captain of the King's Musketeers. For many years, the four friends did not meet each other often. But they did have two more adventures together. Their last adventure was *The Man in the Iron Mask* ...

1

The Bastille, Paris

The year was 1661. It was a warm summer night.
Aramis, the Bishop of Vannes, arrived at the terrible
Bastille prison, in Paris. A guard met him at the gate.

'Take me to Monsieur Baisemeaux,' said Aramis.

A few minutes later, the Bishop was talking to the
governor of the prison. He gave Monsieur Baisemeaux
a paper and he pointed to a name on it.

'I want to see this prisoner,' said Aramis.

The governor read the name on the paper.

'Please follow me, Bishop,' he said.

After a few minutes, the two men arrived at the door
of a cell. The governor opened the door with a key.

'I must talk to the prisoner alone,' the Bishop said.

Aramis went into the cell. The governor shut the
cell door, then he went away.

Aramis looked round the small room. He saw a
young man on a bed. He saw a small window, high in
the wall. He saw a chair, and a plate of food on a small
table. The prisoner had not eaten any of the food.

Aramis looked again at the young man.

'What do you want?' asked the prisoner. Then he looked closely at his visitor. The tall old man was a bishop of the Catholic Church. He was wearing a long purple cloak.

'I've seen you before, Bishop,' the young man said.

Aramis smiled. 'I will tell you a secret,' he said.

'Sit down,' the young man said. 'I'm listening.'

Aramis sat on the chair. After a moment, he began to speak. 'Do you like the Bastille?' he asked. 'Or do you want to be free?'

'What is "free", Bishop?' replied the prisoner.

'A free man sees the flowers growing,' said Aramis. 'He sees the sun shining. He sees the light of the stars. That is freedom!'

The young man thought for a moment. He pointed to some flowers in a vase near his window.

'Here are two roses from the governor's garden,' he said. 'Aren't they beautiful?'

'I have light too,' the prisoner said. 'The sun visits me every day. It comes through my small window. At night, I look at the stars. Am I free, Bishop?'

'Why are you here?' asked Aramis. 'What was your crime?'

'There was no crime,' said the young man. 'But you are going to tell me a secret. What is it?'

Aramis did not answer the young man's question.

'You said, "I've seen you before." And you were right,' the Bishop said. 'You saw me once before. It was in 1646 – about fifteen years ago. You were in your home in the country. I was with a lady in a black dress.'

'I remember her!' said the prisoner. 'After that, she came again with another woman.'

'Yes,' said Aramis. 'And that second woman visited you every month.'

'I remember her visits well,' the young man said. 'After my eighth year, I didn't have any other visitors. I lived in a house with a garden. There were high walls round the garden. I never went outside those walls. Two people took care of me – a nurse and my teacher. My teacher was a very kind man. He told me about my parents. "Your mother and father are dead," he said. Was that true, Bishop? Is my father dead?'

'Yes,' Aramis said.

'And my mother?' the young man asked.

'She is dead *for you*,' Aramis replied.

'But she is alive for others?' asked the young man.

Aramis waited for a moment. 'Yes,' he said.

2
The Prisoner

'Young man, you have a powerful enemy,' said Aramis.

'Yes. My enemy must be a very important person,' said the prisoner. 'I was only a boy, but somebody sent me here. I was fifteen —'

'Did this happen eight years ago?' asked Aramis.

'Yes, it was nearly eight years ago,' the young man replied. 'One day, I was in my room at home. My teacher was in his room, above mine. Suddenly I heard him running down the stairs. He ran into the garden and he called to my nurse. She went into the garden too. The two of them went to the water well. The well was under the windows of my teacher's room.'

'My teacher pointed to the well,' the young man said. 'He was worried. "I've lost the letter from the

Queen!" he told the nurse. "The wind blew it into the well!" My nurse tried to calm him. She told him, "It doesn't matter. The Queen comes here every month. She always burns her letters then – she doesn't keep them. You must write to her. You must tell her about the accident." The nurse wasn't worried.'

'I tried to understand the nurse's words,' the young man said. 'And suddenly, I *did* understand them. A lady came to the house every month. I didn't know her. But I thought, "That lady is the Queen!" I was very surprised!'

'My teacher spoke to the nurse again,' the young man said. 'He told her, "The Queen will not believe me. She always worries about Philippe. Nobody knows about him. Nobody must *ever* know about him. We know that. But does the Queen trust us?" My teacher put his hands over his face.'

'Then, I was *very* surprised,' the prisoner said. 'The nurse and my teacher were talking about *me*, Bishop. My name is Philippe!'

'Then my teacher spoke again,' said Philippe. 'He said, "But you are right. I will write to the Queen today." Then they came back into the house.'

'What happened next?' asked Aramis.

'Some soldiers came to the house,' said Philippe. 'They arrested me. They brought me to the Bastille. I never saw my teacher or the nurse again.'

'The Queen's soldiers killed them,' said Aramis. 'Now I have another question for you. Were there any mirrors in the house with the high walls?'

'Mirrors?' said Philippe. 'What are mirrors? I don't understand the word.'

'A mirror is a piece of glass with shiny metal behind it,' said Aramis. 'You look at a mirror and you see yourself in it.'

'Then the answer is no,' said Philippe. 'There were no mirrors in that house.'

'Ah!' said Aramis. 'How much do you know about the history of our country, Philippe?'

'I know a little about the lives of the kings of France,' said Philippe. 'That is all.'

'Then listen to me,' said Aramis. 'King Louis XIII was the King of France from 1610 to 1643. For a long time, the King and Queen wanted a son. And on the 5th September 1638, Queen Anne gave birth to a boy.'

The Bishop looked at the prisoner carefully.

'The King named the baby boy Louis,' Aramis said. 'He took the boy from the Queen's room. He wanted to show his son to the French people. But an hour later, the Queen gave birth to a *second* son. The Queen's nurse ran to the King and showed the second baby to him. The King was not happy about it.'

'Why not, Bishop?' asked Philippe.

'In France, a king's oldest son becomes the next king. King Louis XIII was afraid. He asked himself, "Which son is the oldest? Will my second son fight my first son? Will the second boy want to be king?" King Louis was very worried.'

'King Louis talked to the Queen's nurse,' Aramis said. 'The nurse took the second boy away from the palace.'

'After that, the boy lived secretly in a house in the country,' said Aramis. 'The nurse went with him and she looked after him. Later, he had a teacher.'

'The people of France never knew anything about this second son,' the Bishop said. 'Now Louis XIII is dead. Louis XIV does not know about the second son. Only Queen Anne, his mother, knows about him. The nurse and the teacher knew about him too, but they are dead.'

'Here is a picture of our King,' said Aramis. He gave a small picture of Louis XIV to Philippe. 'And now, here is a mirror.'

Philippe looked at the picture, then he looked into the mirror.

'The King will never release me from this prison,' Philippe said quietly. 'I will never be a free man.'

'Which *is* the King?' asked Aramis. 'The man in the picture, or the man in the mirror?'

'The King is the man in the Louvre Palace,' said Philippe sadly. 'He is not this man in the Bastille.'

'But I can put *you* in the palace,' said Aramis. 'I can make *you* the King. Then your brother will take your place in prison. And that will be good for the people of France. Your brother is a bad king. He spends money on feasts and expensive clothes. He spends money on houses, horses and women. But his people are poor and hungry. The King does nothing about that.'

Aramis was silent for a moment. Then he spoke again. 'I will see you in this place only once more.'

'When, Bishop?' asked Philippe.

'Soon,' Aramis replied. 'Soon, I and my friends will release you from this prison.'

3

The Louvre, Paris

D'Artagnan was the captain of the King's Musketeers. These men guarded the King. They went everywhere with King Louis.

One morning, D'Artagnan met his friend Porthos at the Louvre, the King's palace in Paris. Porthos was excited.

'I'm going to travel to Vaux next week, D'Artagnan,' he said. 'Monsieur Fouquet, the Chief Minister of Finance, has a fine new house at Vaux. He is going to give a great feast for the King there. He has invited me to the feast. Will you be there, my friend?'

'Yes,' D'Artagnan replied. 'I and my musketeers will be there with the King.'

Half an hour later, D'Artagnan and Porthos met another friend at the Louvre. It was Aramis, the Bishop of Vannes. D'Artagnan was surprised.

'Aramis!' he said. 'Why are *you* at the palace?'

'I wanted to talk to Monsieur Fouquet,' Aramis replied. 'But he is very busy today. He has invited me to the feast at Vaux. I will talk to him there.'

———

Earlier that day, Aramis *had* spoken to Monsieur Fouquet. The King's Chief Minister of Finance was not a happy man.

'My friend,' said Aramis. 'Why are you sad? Everybody is talking about your feast at Vaux. You will make the King very happy.'

'Yes,' said Fouquet. 'The feast will be wonderful. But I have spent all my money on the house at Vaux. I must have more money soon. You gave me a promise, Aramis – a promise of millions of francs.'

'And you will have them soon, my friend,' replied Aramis. 'You'll have the money after the King's visit to Vaux. But now, you must do something for me. I need a written order from you. The order will release a prisoner from the Bastille – a young man. His name is Seldon. The King has sent him to prison for ten years.'

'What was his crime?' asked Fouquet.

'He wrote some unkind words about the bishops of France,' said Aramis. 'But we have forgiven him.'

'There was no other crime?' Fouquet asked.

'There was no other crime,' Aramis replied.

Fouquet went to his desk and he wrote the order on a piece of paper. He gave it to Aramis.

'This will release Seldon,' Fouquet said.

The Bishop smiled. 'Thank you, my friend,' he said.

4
'You Will Be a Great King'

The bell of the Bastille's clock rang nine times. Baisemeaux, the prison governor, had a guest in his room. His guest was the Bishop of Vannes. But Aramis was not dressed in his bishop's clothes. He was dressed in the clothes of a soldier. He was wearing a sword. The two men were drinking wine.

'This is good wine, Baisemeaux!' said Aramis.

'Yes!' said the governor. He drank his wine quickly. Then he called to his servant.

'Bring another bottle!' he shouted.

After an hour, they had drunk several more bottles. The servant came back into the governor's room.

'A messenger has arrived,' the servant said. 'He has brought an order from Monsieur Fouquet.'

The servant gave Baisemeaux a paper. The governor read it. Then he showed it to Aramis.

'It's an order about one of the prisoners,' he said. 'I have to release him. I'll do it tomorrow.'

'My friend!' said Aramis. 'Think of that unhappy man. Release him tonight!'

'You want me to release him now?' said Baisemeaux. 'Very well, my friend. I will do it!'

He left the paper on the table and he went to the door. He called some guards. Quickly, Aramis exchanged the order with a paper from his pocket.

Two prison guards arrived at the door and
Baisemeaux spoke to them. 'Release the prisoner
named Seldon,' he said. 'Bring him here.'

'Seldon?' said Aramis. 'No, no, my friend! The
prisoner's name is Marchiali.'

'Yes, that's right – Marchiali,' said Baisemeaux. 'No!
No ! Not Marchiali! Seldon!'

The wine had given Baisemeaux a headache. He
could not think clearly. He wanted to sleep.

'Look at the order, Baisemeaux,' said Aramis. 'I read
the name Marchiali.'

The governor looked at the paper. 'You're right,' he

said. 'The name *is* Marchiali. You visited that man a few days ago, Bishop.'

———

Ten minutes later, Philippe was standing in the governor's room.

'You are a free man,' Baisemeaux said to him.

Aramis put a hand on Philippe's arm. 'I will help you,' he said to him. 'Come with me, Sir.'

Baisemeaux watched them leave. 'Goodnight,' he said to Aramis. A moment later, he was asleep.

———

Aramis and Philippe left the Bastille in a carriage. The horses pulled it quickly through the dark streets of Paris. Two hours later, it was travelling through the dark forest of Senart. In the middle of the forest, the carriage stopped.

'Soon, we will be at Vaux,' Aramis said to Philippe. 'In the morning, we will go to Monsieur Fouquet's house. But first, we must talk. Don't worry. The driver of the carriage cannot speak or hear.'

'You have the face of your brother, the King,' said Aramis. 'And after tomorrow, *you* will be the King. Louis is going to take your place in prison.'

'Will the people of France let me be their king?' said Philippe. 'My brother, Louis, will be very angry.'

'Who is going to listen to him?' said Aramis. 'Will the walls of the prison listen to him?'

'Louis must not stay in the Bastille,' said Philippe. 'It is a terrible place! He must leave France.'

'You are a good man,' said Aramis. 'And you will be a great king. Sir, I sent a man to the Bastille with some papers and some pictures for you. Did you study them?'

'I studied them and I know them well,' said Philippe. 'I know about Queen Anne, my mother. I know about my family and my ministers.'

'What do you know about Colbert?' asked Aramis.

'Colbert is the Second Minister of Finance,' said Philippe. 'He is an enemy of Fouquet, the Chief Minister of Finance. He wants the King to hate Fouquet.'

'Fouquet is a good man,' said Aramis. 'But he has spent all his money. Soon, you must give him some more. Next, tell me about D'Artagnan.'

'Yes,' said Philippe. 'Your friend D'Artagnan is the captain of the musketeers. Do you want me to send him to prison?'

'No!' said Aramis. 'I will tell D'Artagnan about our plan – but not yet. D'Artagnan is a good man, but he will always fight for the King. Soon, *you* will be the King. Then D'Artagnan will fight for you. But we must be careful. He must not discover our plan now.'

'Bishop,' said Philippe. 'You are going to make me the King of France. What shall I do for *you*? What do you want?'

'Sir,' replied Aramis quietly. 'I am the Bishop of Vannes. But I want to be the Pope in Rome. I will make you the King of France. You must make me the leader of the Catholic Church!'

5

The Great House at Vaux

Everything was ready for the feast at Monsieur Fouquet's house at Vaux. It was the 15th August, and the sun was bright in the sky.

Aramis was talking with Fouquet. The minister was a worried man.

'The King doesn't like me,' he said. 'And I don't like him. But he is my King and he will be my guest. I must try to love that young man.'

'Yes, you must try to love the King,' said Aramis. 'But don't try to love Monsieur Colbert, and don't trust him. He is your enemy!'

'I will take you to your room now, Bishop,' said Fouquet. 'Your room is the Blue Room. It is above the King's room – the Gold Room. Have you brought many servants with you?'

'I have only one servant with me,' said Aramis. 'He will sleep on the floor in my room.'

The King and his mother, Queen Anne, arrived at the great house at Vaux at eight o'clock that evening. The King's ministers and many other important people arrived too. Everybody ate a wonderful meal. Then they listened to music and they watched beautiful fireworks in the gardens. At the end of the evening, everybody received an expensive gift.

After that, the King went to the Gold Room. Fouquet went with him.

'Send Monsieur Colbert here,' the King said to Fouquet. 'I want to speak to him.'

___

That evening, D'Artagnan had visited his friend Aramis in the Blue Room. Porthos was in the bishop's room too, but he was asleep in a chair. He was snoring loudly.

'Aramis, my dear friend!' said D'Artagnan. 'Here we are at Vaux.'

'Yes,' said Aramis. 'Do you like the house?'

'I do,' said D'Artagnan. 'And I like Monsieur Fouquet. But tell me something, Aramis. Why are you having secret meetings with Fouquet? Are you making a plot with him?'

D'Artagnan looked carefully at his friend. 'Aramis,' he said. 'Is the King in danger? Do you want to hurt him? You will have to kill me first!'

'I will never hurt the true King of France,' said Aramis. 'You must believe that, D'Artagnan.'

D'Artagnan smiled. 'Thank you, my friend,' he said. 'Now I must go to my room.'

'Where is that?' asked Aramis.

'It is next to the King's room,' said D'Artagnan.

'Please take Porthos to his own room,' said Aramis. 'I don't want him to sleep here. He makes too much noise!'

———

The two men left the Blue Room. Philippe came from his hiding place behind the bed.

'D'Artagnan is suspicious,' he said to Aramis. 'What are we going to do now?'

'You are going to watch the King,' said Aramis. 'You must watch all his movements. You must learn them.'

'How can I watch him?' Philippe asked.

'There is an opening – here – in the floor,' said Aramis. He pointed to the floor in the middle of the room. Then he lifted a small piece of the wooden floor.

'You can look down into the King's room through this opening,' he said. 'Do you see him?'

Philippe looked down through the opening and he saw his enemy.

'Yes, I see the King,' he said. 'Colbert is with him.'

Aramis and Philippe listened to the conversation in the Gold Room.

'Tell me, Colbert,' the King said. 'Where did Fouquet get the money for this feast? Where did he get the money for this house?'

'From your treasury, Sir,' Colbert replied. 'Thirteen million francs is missing from the treasury.'

'Can you prove that?' asked the King.

'Yes, Sir,' said Colbert. 'You must arrest Fouquet!'

The King was silent for a minute. Then he spoke.

'I will think about this later,' he said.

'Yes, Sir,' said Colbert. But he was angry. He wanted the King to send Fouquet to prison. He wanted to be the King's Chief Minister of Finance.

'Goodnight, Sir,' he said.

Aramis and Philippe watched Colbert leave the King's room. They heard the King call for his servants.

'Now watch again,' Aramis said to the young man. 'Watch his movements and learn!'

———

The next day, the King and all Fouquet's guests enjoyed more music, more fireworks and more food. But in the evening, the King sent for D'Artagnan. Aramis and Philippe listened to the conversation through the opening in the floor.

'How many of your men are here at Vaux?' the King asked D'Artagnan.

'I have the musketeers here, and twenty other guards, Sir,' the captain replied.

'Good! I want you to arrest Monsieur Fouquet,' said the King. 'Do it this evening.'

'You want me to arrest Monsieur Fouquet, Sir?' said D'Artagnan. He was surprised.

'Are you going to say, "I cannot do it", D'Artagnan?' asked the King angrily.

'No, Sir,' answered D'Artagnan, quickly. He moved towards the door, then he stopped.

'I will do it,' he said. 'But please give me a written order for Fouquet's arrest. You are angry now. But soon you will be calm. Then you —'

'Stop!' said the King 'Very well, D'Artagnan. I will think about this again. You will have your written order tomorrow! But watch Fouquet carefully until then. He must not leave the house!'

Suddenly, the King was very tired.

'Please go now, D'Artagnan,' he said.

The captain left the room. The King did not take off his clothes, but he lay down on the huge gold bed. A few minutes later, he was asleep.

6

'I Am the King of France!'

'Am I dreaming?' Louis XIV asked himself.

There were two strange men next to his bed. Each of them wore a black mask and each of them wore a long cloak. One man held a lamp in his hand. The two men were talking quietly.

The King was not dreaming – he had woken. And he was in danger! He jumped from his bed.

'Who are you?' he asked the man with the lamp. 'Are you servants of Monsieur Fouquet?'

'That isn't important,' the man with the lamp replied. 'You must come with us!'

'What do you want?' asked the King.

'You will know that soon,' said the second man. He was very big and tall.

The two men held the King's arms and pulled him to a secret door in the wall of his room. Then they pushed him through the door, and down some stone steps. The King looked around him and he saw wet stone walls. They were in an underground passage!

'Stop!' said the King. 'I will not go with you! I am the King of France!'

'The King!' said the man with the lamp. 'You must try to forget that word, monsieur!'

Then the big man covered the King's mouth with one of his huge hands. He held Louis' arm with his other hand and pushed him along the underground passage. At last, they came to a heavy door in the wall. The man with the lamp opened the door with a key. Suddenly, they were outside the house.

A carriage was waiting under some trees.

The big man pushed the King into the carriage. The man with the lamp got into the carriage too. Then the big man climbed up onto the seat at the front of the carriage. Quietly, he drove it away from Vaux.

———

The carriage arrived at the Bastille prison at about three o'clock in the morning.

The big man spoke to the guards at the gate.

'Wake the governor!' he said.

Five minutes later, Monsieur Baisemeaux came to the gate. The man with the lamp opened the carriage door. He spoke quickly to the big man. The big man got down from the driver's seat and he got into the carriage. He held a gun against the King's head.

'Don't speak. I don't want to shoot you,' he said.

The man with the lamp took off his mask. He walked towards the governor.

'Bishop!' said the governor. 'Why are *you* here?'

'There was a mistake, Monsieur Baisemeaux,' said Aramis. 'You were right two days ago. The order paper was for the release of Seldon, not Marchiali. I've brought Marchiali back to you.'

'This prisoner must not speak to anybody,' Aramis said. 'He is mad. His face is like the King's face – you remember that, Baisemeaux. Now he tells everybody, "I am the King of France." He must talk to nobody – nobody except me, his guard and the King himself!'

Ten minutes later, the King of France was sitting in Philippe's cell in the prison.

———

Aramis and Porthos drove away from the Bastille in the carriage. Soon, they were on the road to Vaux.

And in the great house at Vaux, D'Artagnan was speaking to Fouquet.

'Tomorrow, the King is going to give me orders for your arrest,' he said. 'Until then, I must watch you, monsieur. You must not leave the house.'

7

Louis and Philippe

But there was no reply. No guards came. Louis was angry and frightened. He picked up the chair and he threw it against the wall. For an hour, he shouted and screamed. But then he became calm. He started to think more clearly.

Some hours later, there was a noise outside Louis' cell. Then the door opened and a guard came in with some food.

'You made a lot of noise and you broke your chair,' said the guard. 'Why did you do it, Monsieur Marchiali? You were always a calm and sensible prisoner. Please don't do this again.'

'Listen to me!' said Louis. 'I have a message for the governor. Tell him, "The King of France wants to talk to him." Do it! Do it now!'

The guard laughed. Then he went quickly from the cell and he locked the door.

———

In the great house at Vaux, Philippe was asleep in the King's bed. Night became day, and Aramis came quietly into the room. He woke the young man.

'It is done, Sir,' Aramis told Philippe. 'Everything went well.'

'Where is our friend, Porthos?' asked Philippe. 'He must have a gift. He's going to be a duke.'

Aramis laughed.

'Why are you laughing, Bishop?' said Philippe.

'Oh, Sir!' said Aramis. 'Yes, make Porthos a duke. He'll die of happiness!'

Suddenly, there was a knock at the door.

'D'Artagnan is here,' said Philippe. 'He has come for his orders.'

'You must not talk to D'Artagnan now,' said Aramis. 'He will be suspicious. I will send him away.' He hurried to the door.

D'Artagnan saw Aramis coming out of the King's room. He was surprised.

'Aramis!' he said. 'Why are you here?'

Aramis smiled, but he did not answer the question.

'It is early,' he said. 'The King does not want to talk to anybody now. He is very tired.'

'But the King wanted to talk to me this morning,' said D'Artagnan.

'Come back later, D'Artagnan! Later!' said the King's voice from inside the Gold Room.

Aramis gave D'Artagnan a paper. 'Here is the King's first order for the day,' he said.

D'Artagnan read the paper. 'Oh!' he said.

'I will go with you to Monsieur Fouquet,' said Aramis. 'He will be very happy to see us. Do you understand now, D'Artagnan?'

'Yes,' said the captain of the King's Musketeers. But he thought, 'No, no! I do *not* understand. But I will obey my King!'

D'Artagnan looked carefully at Aramis. 'Tell me,' he said. 'When did you become friends with the King? You've spoken to him only three times in your life!'

'I've spoken to him more than a hundred times,' said Aramis. 'But our meetings were secret!'

8

Fouquet Learns the Secret

Fouquet was waiting in his room. The door opened and Aramis and D'Artagnan came in.

'Monsieur, I am not going to arrest you,' said D'Artagnan. 'The King has given me orders. He thanks you for the feast. He is your good friend.'

Fouquet was surprised. He did not reply.

Then Aramis spoke to D'Artagnan.

'You will be busy this morning, Captain,' he said. 'I will talk with Monsieur Fouquet.'

D'Artagnan said goodbye and he left Aramis and Fouquet alone together. Immediately, Fouquet spoke.

'What is happening?' he asked. 'The King wanted to arrest me, but now I am free. I do not understand.'

'Thirteen million francs is missing from the treasury,' said Aramis. 'The King knows about that. Colbert told him.'

'Yes, the money is missing,' said Fouquet. 'But Louis XIII's finance minister stole the money.'

'The King does not believe that,' Aramis replied. 'The King thinks, "Fouquet is a criminal." And Colbert wants him to think that. Colbert wants to be Chief Minister of Finance.'

'But why am I now a free man?' said Fouquet. 'You have a secret, Bishop. What did the King say to you? Louis doesn't trust you, I know that.'

'The King trusts me now,' said Aramis.

Fouquet began to understand. 'There is a secret between you and the King,' he said. 'Please tell me about it.'

Then Aramis told Fouquet his story. The King's minister listened for a few minutes. But suddenly, he did not want to know more.

'But the King —' he said. He put his hand on his sword.

'Which king?' said Aramis. 'One king hates you, Monsieur Fouquet. The other king likes you.'

'The King – the King of yesterday,' said Fouquet.

'The King of yesterday?' said Aramis. 'Be sure about this. The King of yesterday is in the Bastille. I took him there last night!'

'My God!' said Fouquet. 'That was a crime. A crime against my guest, my King!'

'But King Louis wanted to arrest you,' said Aramis. 'And he wanted to kill you. Now he is in prison, and you are going to live.'

'You are a traitor!' said Fouquet. 'I will kill you!'

He lifted his sword. Then he threw it to the ground.

'No!' he said. 'I can't kill you. You wanted to help me. But I'll go to the Bastille. I'll release the King. You must leave this house, Aramis. And you must leave France. I'll go to Paris now. I will not return for four hours. And in four hours' time, you must be a long way from here.'

'Four hours!' said Aramis.

'You have my promise,' said Fouquet. 'You have four hours. Then the King's soldiers will try to find you. Take my best horses. Ride to the coast. Then take a ship to Belle-Isle. The island is mine. Nobody will hurt you there. Go now!'

Fouquet left the room.

Aramis was angry and unhappy. His plan had not succeeded.

'Shall I go to Belle-Isle alone?' thought Aramis. 'Shall I take Philippe with me? No, I can't do that. Philippe was a prisoner for eight years, and he can be a prisoner again. But I will not leave my dear friend, Porthos. He must come with me.'

The Bishop hurried to Porthos' room.

'Porthos,' he said. 'We're going to leave Vaux now. We're going to ride to the coast. And we're going to ride faster than ever before.'

Porthos put on his cloak and he picked up his sword. Outside the room, the two men met D'Artagnan.

'Are you leaving Vaux?' asked D'Artagnan. 'Where are you going?'

'We have orders from the King, D'Artagnan,' said Aramis. 'Have you spoken to Fouquet?'

'Yes, a few minutes ago,' said D'Artagnan. 'He was in his carriage, on the road.'

'What did he say to you?' asked Aramis.

'He said goodbye,' replied D'Artagnan. 'He said nothing more.'

'Come, Porthos,' said Aramis. 'Are you ready? We must do the King's work.'

9

The Bishop's Plot

Fouquet's carriage went quickly to the Bastille. But the guards at the gate of the prison did not recognize the minister.

'I am Fouquet!' he shouted. 'I am the King's Chief Minister of Finance.'

'It's not true!' shouted one of the guards. 'Monsieur Fouquet is at Vaux!'

Then, Baisemeaux came from his rooms.

'Ah! Minister,' he said. 'I'm sorry. I —'

'It's all right,' Fouquet said. 'Your guards do their job well, Baisemeaux. I will tell the King that. But I want to talk to you.'

He followed the governor to his room.

'Have you seen the Bishop of Vannes in the last few days?' Fouquet asked.

'Yes, monsieur,' said Baisemeaux. 'And he was here last night.'

'Why did you help him with the crime?' asked Fouquet.

'The crime?' said Baisemeaux. 'What crime?'

'The Bishop brought a prisoner here last night,' said Fouquet.

'Yes,' said Baisemeaux. 'That is right.'

'Take me to him immediately,' said Fouquet.

'To Marchiali?' said Baisemeaux.

'Marchiali?' Fouquet said. 'Who is Marchiali?'

'The Bishop's prisoner,' Baisemeaux replied. 'Are you going to take him away? That will make me happy! He screams and he shouts. He shouts, "I am the King of France!" He's a madman.'

'Take me to his cell immediately,' said Fouquet.

'Do you have the order?' asked Baisemeaux.

'What order?' asked Fouquet.

'The order from the King,' said Baisemeaux. 'The Bishop said, "Only I or the King himself must talk to this prisoner." I will take you to the prisoner, but first I must have an order from the King.'

'I will write you an order later,' said Fouquet. 'But take me to the prisoner now! Do you want me to bring ten thousand men and thirty large guns here?'

Baisemeaux was frightened. He took Fouquet along the terrible passages of the prison. Soon, the minister heard the King's voice. The young king was screaming for help. They arrived at the door of his cell.

'Give me the key!' said Fouquet. He took it from the governor. 'Now go! Later, I'll call you. Then you must come back quickly.'

Fouquet put the key into the door. More screams came from inside the cell.

'Help! Help! I am the King of France!' the voice shouted. 'Monsieur Fouquet brought me here! Fouquet must die! The traitor must die!'

The door opened. For a moment, the two men looked at each other. Then the King spoke quietly.

'Are you going to kill me, Fouquet?' he said.

'Sir, don't you recognize your true friend?' Fouquet replied.

'My friend – you!' said Louis.

'Sir,' said Fouquet. 'You are free now.' And he told the King about Aramis' plot.

'I don't believe this story about a twin brother,' said the King. 'It's impossible! These lies are part of the Bishop's plot. Baisemeaux is part of it too.'

'No, Sir,' said Fouquet. 'The Bishop of Vannes tricked the governor. Baisemeaux is an honest man.

But the Bishop prepared his plot carefully. He thought, "Marchiali has the face of the King. The King's ministers, his mother, and his family will believe in him." That is the truth, Sir!'

'Where is the Bishop now?' asked the King.

'He's at my house at Vaux,' replied Fouquet.

'At Vaux!' said the King. 'Have you arrested him?'

'No, Sir. I wanted to release you first,' said Fouquet. 'But now, give me your orders.'

Louis thought for a few seconds. Then he spoke.

'Bring a hundred soldiers here,' he said. 'They will come with us to Vaux. The traitors are going to die.'

'But Sir, is this man, Marchiali, your twin brother?' said Fouquet. 'You cannot kill your brother.'

'I don't believe that story!' said Louis angrily. 'He is *not* my brother! He will die! *All* the traitors will die.'

'Sir,' said Fouquet. 'Please do not kill the Bishop or his friend, Porthos.'

'They *will* die!' replied the King. 'Please do not speak about them again.'

'I'm sorry, Sir,' said Fouquet. 'I must tell you something. I gave the Bishop and his friend my best horses. They are going to escape to my island of Belle-Isle.'

'My Musketeers will capture Belle-Isle,' said the King. 'And they will kill these two traitors!'

Fouquet left the cell and he called the governor.

10

The Brothers

It was late morning. At Vaux, Philippe was wearing King Louis' clothes. He called his servants and he gave them some orders. Next, he had to meet his mother, Queen Anne.

'My brother Louis loves her,' Philippe thought. 'I must love her too. I was a prisoner for many years, but I must try to forgive her for that.'

Queen Anne came to the King's room.

'Louis, my son,' she said. 'What are you going to do about Monsieur Fouquet?'

Philippe kissed the Queen's hand.

'I want you to be friends with Monsieur Fouquet, Mother,' he said.

At that moment, D'Artagnan arrived.

'Captain, where is your friend, the Bishop of Vannes?' Philippe asked him. 'I'm waiting for him, but he hasn't come. Please find him.'

D'Artagnan did not understand.

'The King sent Aramis and Porthos away,' he thought. 'They are doing some secret work for him. Why does he want me to find Aramis now?'

Suddenly there was a sound outside the room. It was the voice of Fouquet.

'This way!' the minister said. 'This way, Sir!'

Everybody turned towards the doorway.

The person in the doorway was King Louis! Fouquet was standing behind him.

Queen Anne screamed.

Louis and Philippe looked at each other. Louis' face and hair were the same as Philippe's. For a moment, Queen Anne did not guess the truth. King Louis moved towards her.

'Mother,' he said. 'Don't you recognize your son?'

Then Philippe spoke.

'Mother,' he said calmly. 'Don't you recognize your son?'

Queen Anne's face became pale. Her body started to shake.

Louis turned to D'Artagnan. He pointed to Philippe's face and then to his own face.

'Captain,' he said. 'One of us has been a prisoner for eight years. The prisoner has not felt the warmth of the sun on his skin. Look at our faces. Who has the palest face? Who has the face of a prisoner – he or I?'

D'Artagnan put his hand on Philippe's shoulder. 'Monsieur,' he said. 'I arrest you. You are my prisoner!'

Philippe did not reply. He looked at his brother again. After a moment, King Louis walked out of the room. Philippe spoke quietly to his mother.

'I am your son,' he said. 'You have made me very unhappy, but I cannot hate you.'

At that moment, Colbert came into the room. He gave a paper to D'Artagnan. The captain of the musketeers read it.

'What is it, Captain?' asked Philippe.

'This is an order from the King,' D'Artagnan said angrily to Philippe. 'Read it.'

Monsieur D'Artagnan

Take the prisoner to the fort on the island of Sainte-Marguerite. Cover the prisoner's face with an iron mask. He must never remove this mask. Nobody must ever see his face again.

Louis

Philippe gave the paper back to D'Artagnan. 'My brother is clever,' he said. 'He is a great man! I am ready.' He smiled sadly.

'You are a great man too, Sir,' said D'Artagnan.

———

Aramis and Porthos rode fast towards the west coast of France. Porthos did not understand the reason for their journey.

'Why did we leave Vaux, Aramis?' he asked. 'The King is going to make me a duke.'

Aramis smiled, but he did not answer.

By evening, the two travellers were at Blois. They were 250 kilometres from the coast and their horses were tired.

'Our friend, Athos, lives near here,' said Aramis. 'We'll visit him. He will give us different horses.'

———

Athos was walking in the garden of his fine house. His servant told him about the arrival of his friends. Athos was pleased to see them.

'You must stay here at my house, my dear friends,' he said.

'Yes!' said Porthos. 'And I must tell you my good news. The King is going to make me a duke.'

Athos was surprised. Aramis put a hand on Athos' arm and the two men moved away from Porthos.

'I must speak to you alone, Athos,' said Aramis very quietly. 'We are in trouble. Porthos doesn't know about it. I made a plot against the King, but the plot did not succeed. Now the King's Musketeers are trying to capture me.'

'But why is the King going to make Porthos a duke?' asked Athos.

'Louis will not make Porthos a duke,' said Aramis. 'Dear Porthos! The plot was mine, but he is in danger too.'

'My dear friend!' said Athos. 'How did this happen? Tell me everything.'

Aramis told his story and Athos listened carefully.

'It was a clever plan, Aramis,' said Athos. 'But – it was a crime!'

'I'm going to take Porthos to Belle-Isle with me,' said Aramis. 'He didn't know about the plot, but the King won't believe that. Will you come to Belle-Isle with us, Athos?'

'No, my friend,' said Athos. 'King Louis is my King. I will not come with you. Do not ask that.'

'Then I'll ask something different,' said Aramis. 'Will you give us your two best horses? We must ride quickly to the coast and our horses are tired.'

'Yes, I'll do that for you,' Athos replied. 'Will you be safe on Belle-Isle?'

'Belle-Isle belongs to Monsieur Fouquet,' Aramis replied. 'The King's soldiers will not attack it.'

'I do not believe that, my friend,' said Athos. 'Be careful! The King is clever and strong.'

11

The Meetings at Nantes

Four weeks had passed. The King was meeting all his ministers in the town of Nantes.

'Where is D'Artagnan?' the King asked Colbert.

At that moment, D'Artagnan entered the room.

'D'Artagnan!' said the King happily.

D'Artagnan was angry. 'Sir, your musketeers have attacked Monsieur Fouquet's family,' he said. 'Did you give them orders about that?'

'No!' said Louis.

'Then the orders came from Monsieur Colbert!' said D'Artagnan. He pointed at Colbert. '*He* gave the orders!'

'What orders?' said Louis. 'Tell me.'

'Somebody gave orders to your musketeers, Sir,' said D'Artagnan. 'They searched Monsieur Fouquet's house. They beat his servants. They arrested his friends and his family.'

'D'Artagnan!' said the King. 'Forget about this! I gave *you* orders. Have you arrested Fouquet?'

'Yes, Sir,' said D'Artagnan.

'Where is he now?' asked the King.

'He is travelling to the Bastille,' D'Artagnan replied.

'Why didn't you go with him?' asked Louis. 'He must not escape.'

'You must understand something, Sir,' said the captain of the musketeers. 'I *want* Monsieur Fouquet to escape. I sent the most stupid of my men as his guards. I cannot be the enemy of Monsieur Fouquet. He is a good man. He released you from the Bastille. You must remember that.'

The King was silent for a minute or two. Then he spoke.

'D'Artagnan, you must go to Belle-Isle today,' he said coldly. 'Take two hundred men with you. You must capture the island and the fort. Don't return here without the keys of the fort at Belle-Isle!'

D'Artagnan left the room and Colbert followed him.

'You have friends on Belle-Isle, D'Artagnan,' the minister said. 'And now you must kill your friends!'

Colbert laughed and he returned to the King.

Fifteen minutes later, D'Artagnan received a written order from King Louis.

> Destroy the fort of Belle-Isle. Nobody must escape. Find the two traitors – the Bishop of Vannes and his friend, Porthos. Find them and kill them.
>
> Louis

12

Belle-Isle

Aramis and Porthos were walking along a beach on Belle-Isle. The beach was near the fort.

'Aramis, please sit down,' Porthos said. 'Sit down and tell me something. Why are we here? Why —?'

'Porthos, what is that, over there?' asked Aramis suddenly. He was pointing out across the sea.

'It's a ship!' said Porthos. 'No – there are five, six, seven ships!'

'Porthos,' said Aramis quickly. 'Those are the King's ships. They are bringing soldiers here. They will attack the island. Tell the islanders about the ships. They must get their guns. They must be ready!'

'I'll do it now, Aramis,' Porthos said. 'But then you must answer my questions.'

He went towards the fort.

Aramis watched the ships coming nearer. Then he saw a small boat leaving one of them. The ships stopped and the small boat sailed towards the island. Some minutes later, the boat arrived at the beach and a young man jumped out of it. Aramis knew the young man. He was a fisherman from Belle-Isle.

At that moment, Porthos returned from the fort.

'Jonathan,' Aramis said to the young fisherman. 'Who sent you here?'

'The King's soldiers sent me,' said Jonathan. 'They took me and my friends from our boat. The captain of the King's Musketeers gave me this letter for you.'

'D'Artagnan!' said Porthos. 'Our friend!'

Aramis read the letter.

> The King has given me orders.
> I must capture Belle-Isle. I
> have arrested Fouquet. He
> is in the Bastille prison. I
> must talk to you.
>
> D'Artagnan.

Aramis' face became pale.

'What is wrong?' asked Porthos.

'Nothing, my friend,' said Aramis. 'Jonathan, did you speak to Monsieur D'Artagnan?'

'Yes, monsieur,' said Jonathan.

'What did he say to you?' asked the Bishop.

'He said, "Bring the Bishop of Vannes and his friend to this ship. I must talk to them." Will you come?' Jonathan said.

'We will not come with you,' Aramis said. 'Return to the ship. Talk to the captain. He must come to the island. We will talk to him here. He must come alone.'

The young man went back to his boat and Porthos and Aramis walked up the stone steps of the fort.

'I don't understand anything!' said Porthos.

'You will soon understand,' Aramis replied.

The two men sat down at the top of the steps. After a few moments silence, Aramis began to speak.

'My friend, I tried to help a young man,' said the Bishop of Vannes. 'I wanted him to take the place of King Louis. But Louis knows about my plot. Now we are both enemies of the King.'

'Oh!' said Porthos. 'This is bad news.'

'Do not worry, Porthos,' said Aramis. 'We are in danger, but we will get out of this trouble. D'Artagnan will help us.'

'I'm not worried about the danger,' said Porthos. 'But I don't like the words, "enemies of the King". The King wanted me to be a duke!'

'The *other* king wanted you to be a duke,' said Aramis.

'Ah! I understand at last,' said Porthos. 'And now I am King Louis' enemy.'

'Oh, I can change that, my friend,' said Aramis. 'I

made the plot. I wanted somebody to help me. I didn't tell you about the plot, but I asked for your help. You remembered our words, "All for one, and one for all", and you came with me. The King will understand that.'

'Look!' said Porthos. 'Somebody is coming from one of the ships. It is D'Artagnan!'

The captain of the musketeers sailed to the beach in a small boat. Then he walked up the steps towards Porthos and Aramis.

'The King is suspicious of me,' he said to them. 'We must be very careful. You are my dearest friends. The King knows that. He will think, "D'Artagnan will try to help his friends. They will try to escape and he will not stop them." The King wants me to kill you. But I will not do that. You must talk to the King. Will you come to the King now?'

'I must stay at Belle-Isle,' said Aramis. 'But you must take Porthos with you. You can help him, D'Artagnan. He was not part of this plot. You must tell the King that.'

'Will you come with me, Porthos, my friend?' asked D'Artagnan.

Porthos looked at Aramis. 'No!' he said.

'Then I have some other plans,' said D'Artagnan. He talked to his friends for a few more minutes. After that, he went back to his boat.

———

D'Artagnan sailed back to his ship and he spoke to his musketeers.

'Gentlemen,' he said to them. 'I went to Belle-Isle. There are many men with guns in the fort. We must capture the island, but it will not be easy.'

'Monsieur,' said one young musketeer. 'You say, "There are many men with guns in the fort." Will these men fight against their King?'

'Belle-Isle belongs to Monsieur Fouquet,' said D'Artagnan. 'Fouquet is not on the island. I arrested him yesterday. But the people on the island do not know that. They are not clever people, but they are Fouquet's men. They love him. They will fight for him. They will not give his island to us. I am going to bring the two chief officers from the fort to this ship. They *are* clever men. I want to talk to them. We will tell them, "Monsieur Fouquet is a prisoner. This is the King's island now." They will send a message to the people in the fort. Then we will take the two men back to the mainland.'

The young musketeer gave D'Artagnan a paper.

'These are my orders from the King, monsieur,' he said. 'Read them.'

D'Artagnan read the paper.

Monsieur D'Artagnan must not bring any officers from the island to the ships.

You must capture the island and you must kill the Bishop of Vannes and his friend.

Louis

D'Artagnan was angry. 'The King did not give his secret orders to me,' he thought. 'He gave them to another soldier.'

'I must go to the King immediately and I must resign from the musketeers,' he said to the soldiers. 'You must all come back to the mainland with me now. We will go to Nantes and the King will give you a new captain. Those are my orders to you, gentlemen!'

The young musketeer stepped forward again. He gave D'Artagnan another paper. The captain read it. His face became pale.

> Monsieur D'Artagnan will resign. He will tell you this immediately. After that, he will no longer be the captain of the musketeers. No man must obey his orders. You must show him this order and you must arrest him. He will be your prisoner. You and three other men must bring him to Nantes. Your soldiers must capture Belle-Isle.
>
> Louis

Ten minutes later, D'Artagnan was in another ship. He heard the first sounds of fighting from Belle-Isle. And an hour later, the ship reached the coast of the mainland.

13

Escape

D'Artagnan had left Belle-Isle. Aramis and Porthos watched his small boat returning to the King's ships. A few minutes later, all the ships started to sail towards the mainland. Aramis turned to his friend.

'D'Artagnan's first plan did not succeed, Porthos,' he said. 'He cannot take us to the mainland. Now he will resign from the musketeers. He will go to the King in Nantes. The ships will go back to the mainland with D'Artagnan. They will not come here again until tomorrow. We will escape tonight! There is a boat inside the Locmaria cave. We will take it. We will go to Spain.'

Suddenly they heard somebody shouting from the fort. 'The soldiers are coming!' the man shouted.

'They didn't go to the mainland,' said Aramis. 'It was a trick!'

Aramis and Porthos looked back to the sea. Near the beach, they saw many small boats. The boats were full of the King's soldiers.

'Get your swords! Get your guns!' Aramis shouted to the islanders.

A few minutes later, the fighting began. The soldiers fought the men of Belle-Isle, and Porthos and Aramis fought against the King's men. It was a long fight, but at last the King's soldiers started to run back to their boats. Aramis and Porthos followed them.

But a few minutes later, the two men heard the sound of guns on the other side of the island.

'Another trick!' said Aramis angrily. 'We were fighting the men at the fort. But at the same time, more soldiers were coming to the other side of the island!'

Soon, all the men and women of the island were running into the fort.

'What shall we do?' they asked Aramis.

'My friends,' said the Bishop. 'The King has arrested Monsieur Fouquet. He is in the Bastille prison. Our friend D'Artagnan told us that. Now you must obey the King's orders. Do not fight the soldiers any more. Put down your guns. Go back peacefully to your homes.'

The people were surprised, but they turned and went quietly away.

'We have saved these people,' said Aramis. 'But the soldiers will try to kill *us*. We must run to the cave now! Our boat is waiting, and there are three friends there. They will help us!'

———

A few minutes later, Aramis and Porthos were in a dark passage at the back of Locmaria cave. They could not see anything.

'Are you there, Yves?' Aramis said quietly. 'Is everything ready?'

'Yes, monsieur,' a voice replied. 'I am here. Jean is here. And his son is with us too.'

Aramis and Porthos walked out of the passage and into the large cave. Yves, Jean, and his son were waiting by a small boat. At the other end of the cave there was an opening – the mouth of the cave. Outside the mouth of the cave was a beach.

'Move the boat out to the sea,' said Aramis.

The three men began to move the boat towards the mouth of the cave. But suddenly there was shouting from the back of the passage.

'My friend,' Aramis said to Porthos. 'Our enemies are coming along the passage. Hide in that corner. The King's soldiers will come out of the passage one by one. Kill them quietly!'

Porthos went to a dark corner on one side of the passage. He picked up a heavy rock. Aramis went to another corner.

Suddenly, an officer walked out of the passage into the cave.

'Now!' said Aramis quietly.

Porthos hit the officer on the head with the rock. The man fell to the ground. He was dead! Aramis pulled him into his corner.

After a few seconds, another soldier followed the officer. 'Now!' said Aramis again.

Ten times Aramis said, 'Now!' Ten times the rock came down. Ten men died!

But a minute or two later, the two friends heard more soldiers arriving in the passage. And a few moments after that, an officer – a captain – came into the cave. He could not see the first group of soldiers, and he could not hear them. He did not understand.

'Where are they?' he asked himself. 'I heard no guns from inside the cave.'

At that moment, a man's huge hand came out from a corner of the cave. The hand went to the captain's neck. And a minute later, the dead officer fell to the ground. But a second officer was close behind him. He saw the captain fall. He shouted to his men.

Aramis and Porthos ran to a large rock. Behind the rock was a heavy wooden barrel of gunpowder.

Rocks began to fall from the roof of the cave. Aramis ran out to the beach. Porthos tried to escape too, but a very large rock fell on him.

'Porthos! Porthos!' Aramis shouted.

The Bishop ran back into the cave, but he was too late. Aramis heard his friend's last cry of pain. Then everything was silent.

Yves, Jean, and Jean's son took Aramis to the boat. They got into it and sailed out from the beach.

'My brave friend is dead,' thought Aramis. 'Dear Porthos! He always wanted to help other people.'

———

An hour later, the little boat was sailing towards Spain.

The three men from Belle-Isle watched Aramis sadly. There were tears in the Bishop's eyes. Soon he was asleep.

14

The Last Musketeer

D'Artagnan was talking with the King in Nantes.

'Sir, you wanted me to kill my friends,' the angry musketeer said. 'That was wrong!'

'But those men put me in the Bastille, my dear D'Artagnan,' said the King. 'Have you forgotten that?'

At that moment, an officer entered the room with a message for the King. The King read it, then he looked at D'Artagnan.

'Monsieur,' he said. 'There has been a battle at Belle-Isle. My soldiers have captured the island.'

'What happened to my friends, Sir?' D'Artagnan asked the King.

'They left the island in a small boat,' said the King. 'You are angry with me, D'Artagnan. But you are a good man. You resigned from my musketeers. I want you to think again about that.'

'I am thinking about the men of Belle-Isle,' replied D'Artagnan. 'They are good men too!'

'Do you want me to release them?' said the King.

'I do, Sir,' said D'Artagnan.

'Very well,' said the King. 'Go now. Tell them, "The King is kind. You are free men." But go quickly. Tomorrow, I will travel to Paris, and I want you to come with me. Tomorrow, you will be the captain of my musketeers again.'

D'Artagnan went quickly to Belle-Isle, but he learnt nothing about his friends. He saw many dead soldiers in the cave. He saw some huge rocks near the mouth of the cave. They had fallen from the roof. He also heard a story about a small boat. The islanders had seen it sailing towards Spain.

The next day, D'Artagnan travelled to Paris with King Louis. But in Paris, D'Artagnan received bad news.

'Sir, my friend Porthos is dead,' D'Artagnan said to the King. 'He died at Belle-Isle. But Aramis escaped.'

'I knew that, D'Artagnan,' the King said quietly.

'You knew it, but you didn't tell me?' said D'Artagnan.

'Yes,' said the King. 'Porthos was killed by a rock at Locmaria. And the Bishop of Vannes escaped to Spain in a small boat.'

'But Sir, how did you know about that?' asked D'Artagnan.

'How did *you* know about it, D'Artagnan?' asked the King.

'I had a letter from Aramis, Sir,' said D'Artagnan. 'He wrote to me from Bayonne, near Spain. I received the letter an hour ago.'

The King took a paper from a box on a table.

'Here is a copy of Aramis' letter,' said the King. 'Monsieur Colbert put it into my hands eight hours ago. D'Artagnan, I *can* bring Aramis back to France. But I'm not going to do that. He will be a free man.'

'Thank you, Sir!' said D'Artagnan quietly.

———

This was the last adventure of the Four Musketeers. A year later, Athos died at his home in Blois. And three years after that, D'Artagnan died too. He was fighting for his king, and he died bravely. His last words were these —

'Athos, Porthos! Soon, I will see you in heaven. Goodbye, until we meet again. Aramis, goodbye for ever!'

Three of the Four Musketeers were dead. Never again did they say, 'All for one, and one for all!'

Published by Macmillan Heinemann ELT
Between Towns Road, Oxford OX4 3PP
Macmillan Heinemann ELT is an imprint of
Macmillan Publishers Limited
Companies and representatives throughout the world

ISBN 0 333 79891 0

This retold version by John Escot for Macmillan Guided Readers
First published 2000
Text © John Escott 2000, 2002
Design and illustration © Macmillan Publishers Limited 1998, 2002
Heinemann is a registered trademark of Reed Educational & Professional Publishing Limited

This version first published 2002

Designed by Sue Vaudin
Illustrated by Kay Dixey
Map on page 3 by Peter Harper
Cover by George Underwood and Marketplace Design

Acknowledgements: The publishers would like to thank Mary Evans
Picture Library for permission to reproduce the picture on page 4.

Printed in China

2004 2003 2002
10 9 8 7 6 5 4 3